Johnny Gruelle

Friendly Fairies

Johnny Gruelle

Friendly Fairies

1st Edition | ISBN: 978-3-75236-004-2

Place of Publication: Frankfurt am Main, Germany

Year of Publication: 2020

Outlook Verlag GmbH, Germany.

FRIENDLY FAIRIES

by

JOHNNY GRUELLE

THE THREE LITTLE GNOMES

A silvery thread of smoke curled up over the trunk of the old tree and floated away through the forest, and tiny voices came from beneath the trunk of the old tree.

Long, long ago, the tree had stood strong and upright and its top branches reached far above any of the other trees in the forest, but the tree had grown so old it began to shiver when the storms howled through the branches. And as each storm came the old tree shook more and more, until finally in one of the fiercest storms it tumbled to the earth with a great crash.

There it lay for centuries, and vines and bushes grew about in a tangled mass until it was almost hidden from view.

Now down beneath the trunk of the fallen tree lived three little gnomes, and it was the smoke from their fire which curled up over the trunk of the old tree and floated away through the forest.

They were preparing dinner and laughing and talking together when they heard the sound of a horn.

"What can it be?" one asked.

"It sounds like the horn of a huntsman!" another cried.

As the sound came nearer, the three little gnomes stamped upon their fire and put it out so that no one would discover their home. Then they climbed upon the trunk of the tree and ran along it to where they could see across an open space in the forest without being seen themselves. And when the sound of the horn drew very close, they saw a little boy climb through the thick bushes.

As the little boy came out into the open space the three little gnomes saw that he was crying.

"He must be lost!" said the first little gnome.

"He looks very tired and hungry!" said the second little gnome.

"Let us go and ask him!" said the third little gnome.

So the three little gnomes scrambled down from the trunk of the fallen tree and went up to where the little boy had thrown himself upon the ground. They stood about him and watched him, for he had put his face in the crook of his arm and was crying.

Finally one of the little gnomes sat down in front of the little boy and spoke to him.

"I am lost!" the little boy said. "My father went hunting yesterday with all his men and when they were out of sight I took my little horn and followed them, but I soon lost their track, and I have wandered about with nothing to eat. Last night I climbed into a tree and slept!"

The three little gnomes wiped the little boy's eyes and led him to their home under the fallen tree. There they finished preparing the dinner and sat about until the little boy had eaten and had fallen asleep.

Then the three little gnomes carried him into their house, away back in the trunk of the tree, and placed him upon one of their little beds.

When the three little gnomes had finished their dinner they lit their pipes and wondered how they might help the little boy find his way home.

"Let us go to old Wizzy Owl and see if he can suggest anything!" said one.

"Yes, brothers," cried another, "Let us go to old Wizzy Owl."

So the three little gnomes went to the home of Wizzy Owl and Wizzy Owl said he would fly high above the forest and try and see the little boy's home.

"I can not see his home!" cried Wizzy Owl. "Maybe Fuzzy Fox can tell you!"

So the three little gnomes went to the home of Fuzzy Fox and Fuzzy Fox said he would run through the forest and see if he could find the little boy's home. So Fuzzy Fox ran through the forest, but could not find the little boy's home. "But," said Fuzzy Fox, "I came upon a wounded deer who told me that a party of huntsmen had passed through the forest yesterday and had shot her with an arrow." So the three little gnomes went to see the wounded deer and they washed the wound the arrow had made and bound it up for her.

Then the three little gnomes sat upon Fuzzy Fox's back and he ran on through the forest with them until they came to a wild boar.

The wild boar had been crippled by the huntsmen, he told the three little gnomes, but had managed to hide himself in the thick bushes and escape. "It must have been the little boy's father and his men," said the wild boar. "I am sorry that I am wounded for I would like to help him!"

Then Fuzzy Fox ran with the three little gnomes through the forest and they met a wounded bear, and a wounded squirrel, and five or six wounded bunny rabbits, and they all told the three little gnomes that the huntsmen had shot them with arrows and that they just managed to escape.

The three little gnomes felt very sorry for their wounded friends and helped them all they could by washing their wounds and tying them up. "We are sorry that we can not go with you and help find the little boy's home," they all said, "For his mother will miss him and cry for him. And we know how much a Mamma or a Daddy can miss a little boy or girl, for we have all grieved for our own little ones that the huntsmen who roam this forest have killed. That is why we feel sorry that we can not help you bring him back to his mother."

8

So Fuzzy Fox ran until he came to the edge of the forest and then the three little gnomes saw a large castle away in the distance with bright red roofs on the tall towers.

"That must be the little boy's home!" said one little gnome.

"Let us return at once to our home under the fallen tree and ask the little boy!" said another. So Fuzzy Fox ran with them back to their home and the little boy told them it was his home.

Then the kind Fuzzy Fox took the three little gnomes and the little boy upon his back and ran to the edge of the forest and on the way they stopped to see the wounded animals, and they were all glad that the little boy's Mamma and Daddy would soon see him. "Oh, if we could only see the children who have been taken away from us by the huntsmen!" they said as they bade the little boy goodbye.

So Fuzzy Fox carried the three little gnomes and the little boy almost to the castle gate and shook hands with him.

"I will remember the way to your home," the boy told the three little gnomes, "and I will be back to see you soon!"

The next day when the three little gnomes were preparing dinner they again heard the little boy's horn, and ran along the trunk of the tree until they came to where they could see across the open space.

Soon there came a great many people, and riding upon a fine horse in front of his Daddy was the little boy, but this day he wore fine silk and satin clothes and they were not torn by the brambles and bushes. Near him rode a beautiful lady. She was the little boy's Mamma.

So the three little gnomes went out to meet them, and the little boy slid from the horse and ran to them and threw his arms around them. "This is my Daddy, and this is my Mamma!" he told them.

The little boy's Mamma and the little boy's Daddy dismounted and came to the three little gnomes and thanked them for returning the little boy to them. "We will give you anything you wish for!" said the little boy's Mamma and Daddy.

"We wish for nothing!" said the three little gnomes, "We live happily here in the forest and our wants are simple, but if you could send us some clean white cloths to bind up the wounds you give our forest friends we would be very grateful!"

"I told Daddy of the wounded creatures!" said the little boy. "Yes," his Daddy said, "and I have given orders that no one in my country shall hunt through this forest, and from now on your forest friends will be unmolested and can always live here in peace and happiness." For the great king was sorry that he or his men had ever caused any of the forest creatures any sorrow. And after that the creatures of the forest were never harmed and they grew up so tame they would wander right up to the castle, where the king's men would feed them.

The tiny thread of smoke still curls up over the trunk of the fallen tree, and the voices of the little boy and his Daddy mingle with the tiny voices of the three little gnomes as they prepare their dinner; for the great King and the little Prince come often to visit their friends, the three little gnomes.

THE HAPPY RATTLE

Willie Woodchuck sat at the entrance of his burrow home whittling upon a tiny dried gourd.

"What are you making?" asked Timothy Toad, as he hopped through the grass and sat in front of Willie.

"Oh, I am just whittling because I have nothing else to do!" replied Willie Woodchuck.

So Timothy Toad hopped on down the path until he met Eddie Elf.

"Willie Woodchuck is whittling because he has nothing else to do!" said Timothy Toad.

"I will stop by and see him!" said Eddie Elf. So Timothy Toad hopped along the path until he met Gerty Gartersnake.

"Willie Woodchuck is whittling because he has nothing better to do!" said Timothy Toad.

"I will go down that way and see him!" said Gerty Gartersnake, and she started down the path.

So Timothy Toad hopped down the path until he met Wallie Woodpecker. "Willie Woodchuck is whittling because he has nothing better to do!" said Timothy Toad.

"I will fly down and see him!" said Wallie Woodpecker, and away he flew. Timothy Toad hopped on down the road until he met Billie Bumblebee.

"Willie Woodchuck is whittling because he has nothing else to do!" said Timothy Toad.

"I will buzz down that way and see him!" said Billie Bumblebee, as he buzzed away.

When Timothy Toad arrived at his home his wife, Tilly Toad, was sweeping off the front steps. "What do you think, Tilly?" Timothy Toad cried, "Willie Woodchuck is, whittling because he has nothing else to do!"

"Dear me! You don't say so!" cried Tilly Toad, as she stood her broom in the corner and started down the path. "I will hop down and see him!" she said.

"I will hop back with you, Tilly!" said Timothy Toad.

They had not hopped far before they met Eddie Elf, who was singing happily to himself as he walked along. "Willie Woodchuck is whittling on a rattle!" he said, when the two Toads stopped him.

"We are hopping back to see him," said Tilly and Timothy Toad. "I will go back with you!" said Eddie Elf.

They had not gone far until they met Gerty Gartersnake, singing away very happily. "Willie Woodchuck is whittling on a beautiful red and black rattle!" said Gerty Gartersnake.

"We are going back to see him!" said Tilly and Timothy Toad and Eddie Elf.

"Then I will go back with you!" said Gerty Gartersnake.

They had not gone far until they met Wallie Woodpecker, who also was singing happily. "Willie Woodchuck is whittling on a rattle and it is blue, red and black and rattles beautifully."

"We are going back to see him!" said Tilly and Timothy Toad and Eddie

Elf and Gerty Gartersnake.

"Then I will go back with you!" said Wallie Woodpecker.

They had not gone far before they met Billie Bumblebee. "Willie Woodchuck is whittling on a beautiful yellow and blue and red and black rattle and it rattles beautifully."

"We are going back to see him!" said Tilly and Timothy Toad and Eddie Elf and Gerty Gartersnake and Wallie Woodpecker.

"Then I will go back with you!" said Billie Bumblebee, so away they all went until they came to Willie Woodchuck's home.

"Where is Willie Woodchuck?" they asked of Winnie Woodchuck, his wife.

"He has taken his beautiful new yellow and red and blue and black and white rattle, which rattles so beautifully, over to show to Grumpy Grundy, the Owl!" said Winnie Woodchuck.

"Then we will go there!" said the others.

"Then I will go with you!" said Winnie Woodchuck.

Grumpy Grundy, the Owl, was a very cross old creature, and if everything did not go to suit her all the time, she hooted and howled; in fact she had cried so much she had made large red rings around her eyes.

When Tilly and Timothy Toad and Eddie Elf and Gerty Gartersnake and Wallie Woodpecker and Billie Bumblebee and Winnie Woodchuck arrived at Grumpy Grundy's place they heard merry laughter and whenever the laughter ceased, they heard the buzz and rattle and hum of Willie Woodchuck's rattle.

So they went inside.

And there was Willie Woodchuck with the beautiful yellow and red and blue and black and white rattle, and when he rattled it Grumpy Grundy rolled on the floor and laughed until the tears ran from her eyes.

So they all lifted Grumpy Grundy on a chair and wiped her eyes and what do you think! the red rings around them were wiped away and she looked young and pretty again.

"Oh dear!" said Grumpy Grundy, the Owl. "I have never enjoyed myself so much before, and I will never be grumpy and be called a Grundy again! No sir! never!" and her eyes twinkled with merriment.

And all were greatly pleased at the great change in Grumpy Grundy.

Eddie Elf laughed, Tilly and Timothy Toad chuckled, Gerty Gartersnake giggled, Wallie Woodpecker beat a tattoo on wood, Billie Bumblebee buzzed and Winnie Woodchuck sang a woodchuck song.

And after that no one could say that Willie Woodchuck had nothing else to do, for he spent his time making beautiful "happy rattles" which he gave away to all the creatures, and everyone laughed and made merry whenever they heard the beautiful yellow and red and blue and black and white rattles which rattled so beautifully and drove away the grumpies.

RECIPE FOR A HAPPY DAY

One morning Marjorie's Mamma called to her several times before Marjorie answered, for her pretty brown eyes were very sleepy and would hardly stay open.

"Come, dear! Please hurry, for I want you to run to the grocery before breakfast!" Mamma called from the foot of the stairs.

"Oh dear!" exclaimed Marjorie, "I don't want to get up!" and keeping her head on the pillow just as long as she could Marjorie crawled out of bed backwards.

Her clothes were scattered about the room and her stockings were turned inside out. Her dress would not fasten and she cried, so that Mamma had to come upstairs and dress her.

So you see Marjorie's day began all wrong, for everything started topsy-turvy.

"Now hurry, dear!" Mamma said as she handed Marjorie the basket.

Marjorie slammed the door as she went out and she was so cross she did not notice the beautiful sunshine nor hear the pretty songs which greeted her from the tree tops.

"It's so far to the old store!" Marjorie grumbled to herself, as she pouted her pretty lips and shuffled her feet along the path.

"Hello, Marjorie!" laughed a merry voice.

Marjorie saw a queer little elf sitting upon a stone at the side of the road. His little green suit was so near the color of the leaves Marjorie could scarcely distinguish him from the foliage. He wore a funny little pointed cap of a brilliant red, and sticking in it was a long yellow feather.

Two long hairs grew from his eyebrows and curled over his cap. He was hardly as large as Marjorie's doll, Jane.

"Who are you, and where did you come from?" Marjorie cried, for she thought him the most comical little creature she had ever seen.

"Why, I'm Merry Chuckle from Make-Believe Land!" replied the elf. "And aren't you very cross this lovely day?"

"I did not want to get up!" cried Marjorie, "and I just hate to go to the store! It's too far!" She dropped her basket on the ground and sat down beside the elf on the large stone.

"Isn't it funny?" laughed Merry Chuckle. "There are hundreds of children just like you who make hard work of getting up when they are called in the morning and who remain cross and ugly all day long!"

"I really do not mean to be cross, but I just can't help it sometimes!" Marjorie said.

"Oh, but indeed you can help it, Marjorie!" the elf solemnly said as he shook his tiny finger at her nose. "And I am going to tell you how. First of all, when you awaken in the morning you must say to yourself, 'Oh what a lovely, happy day this is going to be!' then raise your arms above your head and take three long, deep breaths. Jump out of bed quickly, always remembering to put your toes on the floor first.

"For," continued Merry Chuckle, "Old Witchy Crosspatch is always waiting for children to get out of bed backwards. And when they do, she catches them by the heels and turns everything topsy-turvy all day long; but when you get out of bed toes first, I'll be there to start you on a pleasant day and Witchy Crosspatch will have to return to Make-Believe Land and hide her head!" "Sure enough, I did crawl out of bed backwards this morning!" Marjorie said.

"I know you did, my dear!" Merry Chuckle giggled. "And every time you do old Witchy Crosspatch makes everything seem disagreeable!"

"But I hate to run errands, Mister Chuckle!" cried Marjorie. "The old road is so dreadfully long and tiresome!"

"But the longer the road the more happiness you can find along the way, my dear!" Merry Chuckle replied, quick as a wink, his little eyes twinkling brightly. "If you look up at the blue sky and the beautiful sunshine and sing with the birds as you run along you'll find the road seems too short and you'll be back before you notice it. Just try it and see."

So Marjorie looked up the road with a smile and, sure enough, it did not seem so far to the store, and when she turned around, she was sitting upon the stone alone. The little elf had suddenly disappeared. Marjorie picked up her basket and skipped down the road singing at the top of her voice and before she had time to think about how far it was she was back home telling Mamma all about the queer little elf from Make-Believe Land.

"You haven't been away long enough to stop and talk with anyone on the road!" laughed Mamma. "Are you sure you have not been dreaming?" Marjorie wondered if it really had only been a dream, but the next morning when the golden sunshine peeped through her bedroom curtains, Marjorie did as Merry Chuckle had told her the day before. First of all she woke up and cried, "Oh what a lovely day this is going to be!" Then she took three long, deep breaths and then she jumped out of bed quickly, right on her toes. And, sure enough, old Witchy Crosspatch had to go back to Make-Believe Land and hide her head, so Marjorie spent a lovely, happy day with Merry Chuckle.

"I hope all children will hear of my recipe for a joyous day," said Merry Chuckle, "so that each day for them can be filled with sunshine and happiness!"

GRANDFATHER SKEETER-HAWK'S STORY

It was a beautiful day in the late summer. Tommy Grasshopper, Johnny Cricket and Willy Ladybug were playing on a high bank of the river, and watching the little fish jumping after tiny flies and bugs that fell upon the surface of the stream.

"Let's go up higher so that we can see them better," Willy Ladybug said.

"Yes, let's climb up on the tall reeds so that we can look right down in the water," Johnny Cricket said. "But we must be very careful and not fall, for the fish would soon swallow us, and that would not be very much fun!" he laughed.

So Tommy Grasshopper and Johnny Cricket caught hold of Willy Ladybug's four little hands and helped him to climb up the tall reeds, for Willy was not as old as the other Bug Boys, and might fall in the water if they did not help him.

From the tall reeds the three Bug Boys could look down in the water and see the pretty little sun fish and the long slim pickerel darting around and turning their shiny sides so that the sun would reflect its rays on them, just as if they were looking glasses.

The Bug Boys watched the fish until they grew tired, and they were just starting down the tall reed when a great big dragon fly flew upon the top of the reed and called to them.

Of course all the Bug Boys knew old Gran'pa Skeeterhawk—for it was he —so the three returned to the reed and sat down again to pass the time of day with Gran'pa.

Presently Willy Ladybug saw a strange fish in the water.

"What kind of a fish is that, Gran'pa Skeeterhawk?" he asked.

"That's a catfish!" Gran'pa replied. "Queer looking fish, the catfish are; they do most of their feeding at night since Omasko, the elk, flattened their heads."

"Dear me! Are their heads flat?" Johnny Cricket asked.

"Flat as a pancake!" Gran'pa Skeeterhawk replied, and then told them this story:

"I've heard *my* Gran'pa tell that once the catfish had heads that were shaped like sunfish," Gran'pa Skeeterhawk said, "and they thought that they were not only the most beautiful fish but the fiercest fighters in the world, although they would always swim away as fast as they could whenever anything came near them. You see, they really were not even a teeney, weeney bit brave.

"But when the catfish got by themselves and they thought there was no one else to overhear them, they would make up fairy tales of wonderful adventures they had gone through, and fierce monsters they had destroyed. One would say 'I wish I were large enough to drag home the enormous giant eel I killed today. He was sixteen feet long, and weighed five hundred pounds.' Another would say, 'Pooh, that is nothing! Why, you ought to see an Indian who tried to catch me in a net! Why, I not only pulled him in the water and dragged him all over the bottom, but I made him promise he would never disturb any of the catfish tribe after this!'

"Just then a little bird flew over the water and his shadow so startled the boastful catfish, they buried themselves in the mud at the bottom of the stream.

"After a while," Grand'pa Skeeterhawk continued, "They got up courage to peek out of the mud, and as they saw nothing to frighten them, they formed in a circle and told more tales of their fighting qualities.

"One old catfish who had been the leader because he could tell the biggest tales and hide under the mud quicker than any of the others finally said: 'We are the best fish in the water, as you all know, so I think it will be a good plan to fight everything that comes near the water from the land!'

"'Shall we fight the big hawk who wades in the water and catches some of us?' asked a little kitten fish.

"'Kitten fish should be seen and not heard!' the old chief catfish answered quickly. I do not believe we should harm the hawk. He is not large enough. I was thinking of the large beast who comes wading along the shores and eats the grasses that grow beneath the surface. You know he has to raise his head every once-in-a-while in order to breathe, so if we should all hang on to him we could pull him under the water.'

"So the catfish, although they were so frightened that their fins grew stiff, decided that they would follow their chief, for they expected he would be the first to hide under the mud when the big beast came.

"Finally old Omasko, the elk, came down to the river to feed, and the old chief catfish swam out and pulled on Omasko's whiskers, and all the other catfish cried: 'See how brave and fearless the mighty catfish are!' and they all swam out and pulled Omasko's whiskers, too. This made Omasko very angry, for he never harmed any fish in his life.

"He began jumping and pawing with his heavy hoofs, and smashed all the catfish down in the mud and when they finally came out again, which was not until two or three days later, their heads were as flat as they are now!

"That is why all catfish have flat heads," Grandfather Skeeterhawk finished.

"It served them right for being so boastful!" Johnny Cricket said.

"It served them right for trying to harm someone who never harmed them!" Gran'pa Skeeterhawk replied, as he darted up in the air and flew over the tall cat-tails.

CROW TALK

"Caw, Caw, Caw," one old crow cried as he faced the other two crows. "Caw?" asked the second old crow as he plumed his feathers and screwed his head around to get a better view of the little boy lying under the tree.

"Caw-AAAAH! Ca—aaaaw!" replied the first crow.

"Those crows must be talking to each other!" Dickie Dorn thought to himself, as he lay upon his back under the big oak tree and watched the three crows.

The third crow now cried, "Awww! Ca-ca-caw!"

Dickie jumped up and ran down the hill to where Granny lived. It was a tiny little house, not much larger than a piano box, but it was plenty large enough for Granny, for Granny was only two feet high. Some people even thought Granny was a witch.

Of course Dickie knew that Granny was not a witch, for Granny was very good and kind. So Dickie knocked at Granny's tiny front door.

"Come in!" Granny cried. "Good morning, Dickie!" she said, as Dickie crawled into the tiny living room.

When Dickie took a seat upon a tiny sofa he did not know just how to ask Granny for what he wanted, so he twiddled his thumbs.

"Why do you twiddle your thumbs, Dickie?" Granny asked, as she smiled through her glasses at him.

"I was wondering what the three crows were talking of!" Dickie replied. Granny went to her tiny cupboard and brought out a little bottle of purple fluid. She dropped three drops of this into a tiny spoon and held it to Dickie.

"Am I to take it, Granny?"

"Yes, my dear, and you will be able to understand what the three crows are talking about."

Dickie swallowed the purple fluid, for he was very anxious to return to the big oak tree and listen to the crows. Granny watched him for a few moments with her eyes full of twinkles, then she told him to run along to the tree.

And Dickie thanked Granny and ran as fast as he could to the tree where the three crows were still talking.

The first crow cried, "I know where there is a box filled with golden pennies!"

"Ah, my brother, where?" asked the second crow.

"In the middle of the great meadow, and it will belong to the one who finds it first!"

"I know where there is a box full of candy!" the third crow cried.

"Ahhhh! Where is it, my brother?" asked the first crow.

"In the middle of the great meadow, and it will belong to the one who finds it first."

"I know where there is a box full of ice cream!" cried the second crow.

"Aha! My brother, where?" asked the third crow.

"In the middle of the great meadow, and it will belong to the one who finds it first!"

Then the crows went on talking about other things, but Dickie did not hear them, for he was running in the direction of the great meadow as fast as he could.

And when he came to the middle of the great meadow there was a large box, and in the large box were three other boxes. One contained the golden pennies, another the candy and the third was full of ice cream.

"I found it first!" Dickie cried and he took a pencil stub from his pocket and, with much twisting of mouth and thinking, he printed his name upon the box.

Then Dickie ran home as fast as he could and told Daddy Dorn. Daddy Dorn hitched up Dobbin Dorn and Dickie and Daddy went to the middle of the great meadow and put the big box in the wagon and took it home.

Then they called Mamma Dorn and they all ate some of the ice cream and candy. Then Dickie took some of the ice cream and candy and some of the golden pennies to Granny.

Then Dickie ran back home and had some more ice cream and candy, and asked Daddy if he might take some of the golden pennies downtown and buy something, and Daddy Dorn said: "Of course, Dickie Dorn, for they are your golden pennies." So Dickie took two handfuls of the golden pennies downtown and bought a fine little pony with a little round stomach, and he bought a pretty pony cart and harness. Then Dicky drove the pony back home.

By the time Dickie reached home he was hungry for more ice cream and candy, so he went to the box to get some. "Oh Mamma and Daddy!" he cried, "Come see! The box is full of candy and ice cream!" And sure enough that was the case, for although they had eaten almost all of the ice cream and candy before now the two boxes were filled again. Then Daddy Dorn took two large handfuls of golden pennies from the golden penny box and they watched the box fill up with pennies again.

"Whee!" cried Dickie Dorn. "Whee!" cried Mamma Dorn, and "Whee!"

cried Daddy Dorn. "We will give a party!" So Dickie drove around to everybody's house in his pony cart and invited everybody to come to the party.

And they all had such a nice time they ate the ice cream box empty sixteen times and it filled right up again, and they ate the candy box empty seventeen times and it filled right up again, and Dickie and Mamma and Daddy Dorn gave everybody all the golden pennies they could carry home and emptied the penny box eighteen times, and whenever they emptied the golden penny box it filled right up again.

And every one felt very grateful to Dickie Dorn and thanked him for such a nice time, and Dickie brought Granny out of a corner where she was eating her eighth dish of ice cream and told everybody that it was Granny who had really given the party, and he told them how Granny had helped him to learn crow talk.

So the people never called Granny a witch after that, for they knew she was very good and kindly.

And Dickie put the three boxes—the candy box, the ice cream box and the box with the golden pennies—out in front of his house so that whenever anyone wished candy or ice cream or golden pennies they might walk up and help themselves.

Dickie Dorn calls it an "All-The-Time Party," for there is always someone out in front of Dickie Dorn's house eating from the candy and the ice cream box and filling their pockets with golden pennies.

Some day I hope to see you there.

THE FAIRY RING

A little old man with a violin tucked under his arm shuffled down the attic steps and the many flights of stairs until finally he reached the streets.

As he shuffled down the street, he clutched his coat tightly about his throat, for the air was chill and he felt the cold.

At the first street corner he stopped and placed his violin to his shoulder to play, but catching a glance from the policeman across the street he hastily tucked his violin under his arm and shuffled on.

He walked a great distance before he again stopped.

It was a busy corner where hundreds of people passed every few minutes, but when he played no one stopped to listen to his music, much less to drop anything in the tiny tin cup he had placed on the sidewalk before him.

Tears came to the poor little old man's eyes; everyone was too busy to stop to hear his music.

So in the evening when he slowly retraced his steps towards his attic home, his feet were very tired and he shuffled more than he had in the morning. His back humped and his head drooped more, and the tears nearly blinded him. He had to stop and rest at each flight of stairs and he fell to his knees just as he reached the attic door.

He sat there and rested awhile, then caught hold of the doorknob and raised himself to his feet.

A quaint little white-haired woman greeted him with a cheery smile as he entered, then, seeing his sad face, she turned her head and tears came to her eyes.

"Honey!" the little old man sobbed, as he stumbled towards her chair and fell to his knees before her, burying his face in her lap.

Neither could say a word for a long time, then the little old man told her he had been unable to make a single penny by playing.

"No one cares to hear an old man play the violin!" he said. "No one cares that we go hungry and cold! And I can still play," he added fiercely, "just as well as ever I could! Listen to this!" and the little old man stood up and drew his bow across the violin strings in a sure, fiery manner, so that the lamp chimney rattled and sang with the vibrations of the strings.

And in his fierceness he improvised a melody so wild and beautiful his sister sat entranced.

As the little old man finished the melody he stood still more upright. Then straightening his old shoulders and pulling his hat firmly on his head, he stooped and kissed the old lady and walked with a firm tread to the door.

"I shall make them take notice tonight!" he cried. "I shall return with success!"

So again he went down the long flights of stairs and down the street until he came to a good corner where traffic was heavy.

There, with the mood upon him which had fired him in the attic, he played again the wild melody.

A few people hesitated as they passed, but only one stopped. This was an old woman, bent and wrinkled, who helped herself along with a cane. She stopped and looked him squarely in the eye and the little old man felt he should recognize her, but he could not remember where he had seen her before, nor was he sure that he had ever looked upon her until now.

At any rate, the faint memory inspired him and, raising his violin, he played a beautiful lullaby.

Before he had finished the old woman leaned over and dropped something into his little tin cup.

It sounded as loud as a silver dollar would have sounded.

"The dear old generous soul!" the old man thought as he continued playing.

He played for hours, but the old woman was the only one who stopped. "I will at least have enough to get Cynthia some warm food!" he said, thinking of what the old lady had dropped into his tin cup.

But when he looked, what was his dismay to see only a large iron ring!

Again he climbed the stairs to the attic but he felt too weary to say a thing and his sister knew that he had met with disappointment. He tossed the iron ring to her lap and went over to the bed and threw himself upon it.

"This is the end!" he said, and told her about the iron ring.

"The old woman seemed interested in my playing!" he said, "And perhaps she gave all she could give!"

"Let us not be downhearted, Brother!" said the sister. "Surely tomorrow you will find someone who will reward your talent!"

The little old man was quiet for a long time and then he arose and again drew his bow across the violin strings. The old lady sat very still and dreamed, for her brother was playing one of their childhood songs.

As she lost herself in reverie, she turned the iron ring around her finger and saw upon its surface, as she turned it, the faces of her playmates of long ago.

And as the brother swept from one melody to another, she saw the iron ring change color and grow larger and larger.

And, as she turned it, she saw the figures of her childhood playmates turn before her upon her lap, and they joined their voices with the silvery notes of the violin's long ago songs until the attic was filled with the melody and the figures danced from her lap and, taking her by the hand, circled in the center of the attic room laughing and singing.

The little old man had been playing with his eyes closed, but as the songs grew louder he opened them and beheld the ring of little figures, with his sister holding hands with two of them. And, rising from the bed, still playing the childhood songs of long ago, he walked to the center of the room. As he did so, the figures rose in the air and seemed to grow lighter and larger. And suddenly the scene changed! He was out in the woods, with lofty trees towering above him, while all about, laughing and talking, were hundreds of little fairies, gnomes and sprites, and there, too, were the playmates of long ago, just as he had seen them when he had closed his eyes and played in the attic.

And there, too, was his sister as she had been when a child. He looked at himself, and lo! he was no longer wrinkled and old. He was young again!

In his gladness he danced with joy, and catching his sister to his breast he kissed her again and again.

And, looking about him with shining eyes, he again drew his bow across the strings and played a tune so lively and full of sweet happiness the childhood friends caught hands and danced in a circle, and the little sprites, elves, gnomes and fairies caught hands and danced around the children, and as they passed before the brother he caught a mischievous glance from the eyes of one of the little fairies, and he knew in a moment she was the one who had played the old woman, and who had given him the iron ring....

The people who lived in the room below the attic room missed the little old man's shuffling step, and, not hearing it for two days, they told the landlady, a kindly soul who had let the brother and sister have the attic room free of charge, and all went up to investigate....

They rapped upon the attic door. All was quiet within. Timidly they opened the door and looked in. There upon the floor lay an old rusty iron ring. It was the Fairy Ring.

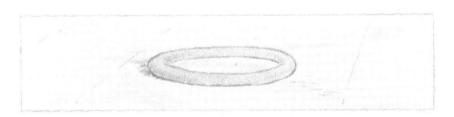

MR. AND MRS. THUMBKINS

Thumbkins ran beneath the bushes and down the tiny path until he came to where Tommy Grasshopper sat upon a blade of grass swinging in the breeze.

"Have you seen Mrs. Thumbkins, Tommy Grasshopper?" Thumbkins called.

"I have been asleep," replied Tommy Grasshopper, "And I haven't seen her!"

"Oh dear! Oh dear!" cried Thumbkins. "She has not been home all day!"

"Perhaps she went over to see Granpa Tobackyworm!" suggested Tommy Grasshopper, as he flicked his wings and made the blade of grass swing up and down.

So Thumbkins thanked Tommy Grasshopper and ran over to Granpa Tobacyworm's house.

Granpa Tobackyworm was sitting upon a blade of grass, swinging in the breeze and smoking his old clay pipe.

"Oh, Granpa Tobackyworm! Have you seen Mrs. Thumbkins? She has not been at home all day and I can not find her!" cried Thumbkins.

"Yes, I saw her early this morning going down the path with her acorn basket," said Granpa Tobackyworm as he blew a few rings of smoke in the air. "Perhaps she has gone to the Katydid grocery store to buy something," Granpa Tobackyworm added as he bounced up and down on his blade of grass.

So Thumbkins thanked Granpa Tobackyworm and went on down the tiny path.

"Hello, Thumbkins!" cried a cheery voice as Thumbkins ran under a bunch of flowers. "Where are you going in such a hurry?"

Thumbkins saw Billy Bumblebee sitting upon one of the flowers, swinging in the breeze.

"Mrs. Thumbkins has not been home all day!" said Thumbkins. "And I can not find her anywhere!"

"HUMMMM!" replied Billy Bumblebee. "Let me think! HUMMMM!" This was his way of thinking very hard.

"Perhaps she has gone over to see Granpa Tobackyworm, Mr Thumbkins!"

"No!" replied Thumbkins, "I went there, and also over to the Katydid store, but she was not there!"

"Suppose you climb upon my back, Thumbkins, and let me help you find her!" said Billy Bumblebee, as he buzzed his wings, making the flower sway up and down. So Thumbkins climbed up the flower stalk and took a seat upon Billy Bumblebee's back.

"Let us fly way up in the air so that we may look down over all the

48

country!" said Billy Bumblebee, as he made his wings whirr and climbed high in the air.

Billy Bumblebee and Thumbkins looked over the country carefully, but they could not see Mrs. Thumbkins anywhere.

Finally Billy's sharp eyes discovered something shiny down by the side of the pond, so they flew down towards it. It was a new tin can house. The door was closed.

Thumbkins alighted from Billy Bumblebee's back and knocked at the door.

TINKY-TINKY-TINK!

"GRUMP! GRUMP!" said a deep voice from inside the tin can house. Billy Bumblebee peeped through a chink in a window, and saw a hoppy-toad with his mouth full of pancakes.

So Thumbkins picked up a pebble and knocked louder. TONKY-TONKY-TONK!

Old Man Hoppy-toad came to the door with a pancake in each hand and another large one in his mouth. "GRUMP! GRUMP!" he said.

"Where is Mrs. Thumbkins?" Billy Bumblebee demanded, as he buzzed around Old Man Hoppy-toad's head.

"I don't know!" said Old Man Hoppy-toad when he had swallowed the pancake.

"Yes, you do!" Thumbkins cried as he caught Old Man Hoppy-toad's hand. "Who made those pancakes for you?"

Billy Bumblebee buzzed closer to Old Man Hoppy-toad's head and Old

Man Hoppy-toad blinked his big round eyes and finally said, "She is locked up in the kitchen!"

So Thumbkins ran to the kitchen and came out with Mrs. Thumbkins. Old Man Hoppy-toad had locked her in the kitchen so she would have to bake lots and lots of pancakes for him.

Thumbkins was so glad to see Mrs. Thumbkins he came very near crying. And Billy Bumblebee said to Old Man Hoppy-toad, "Now you must leave our neighborhood, for we do not permit anyone to bother anyone else in the Town of Tinythings."

So Old Man Hoppy-toad had to pack up all his things in a red handkerchief and hustle out of town.

And Billy Bumblebee buzzed right around his head as Old Man Hoppy-toad went down the path "Lickity split-Hoppity hop!" and never once looked behind him.

JOHNNY GRUELLE

Thumbkins and Mrs. Thumbkins went back home, and when Billy Bumblebee returned and told them he had made Old Man Hoppy-toad go 'way down to the river they knew they would never be troubled with him again.

Mrs. Thumbkins said she had fried pancakes all day but she was not too tired to fry more. So she made a lot of pancakes, while Billy Bumblebee flew home and returned with a bucket of honey, and they had so many pancakes Mrs. Thumbkins asked Billy Bumblebee if he would fly around and invite all the neighbors in to help eat them.

Tommy Grasshopper, Granpa Tobackyworm, and all the other friends of the Thumbkins came and ate the lovely pancakes, covered with the delicious honey.

And, after eating as much as they could, everybody caught hold of hands and danced until late in the night, for the Katydid orchestra was there to furnish the music.

THE OLD, ROUGH STONE AND THE GNARLED TREE

A great rough stone lay beneath a gnarled old tree. Years ago a tiny squirrel had climbed upon the stone to nibble some nuts, but before he had finished he was startled away.

"There!" thought the stone to himself as he saw a nut roll to the ground, "now that nut will take root and grow into a tree and I will have to lie here for ages beneath its branches. I wish the silly squirrel had gone some other place to eat the nuts!"

When the little nut took root and sent its tiny shoots up in the air, the old, rough Stone said, "There! I knew it!" and he disliked the tree from that time on.

The old, rough Stone watched the tiny green shoot grow and grow until it grew into an enormous tree.

"Just see how he pushes me up in the air with his roots!" the old, rough Stone said to himself.

When the gnarled tree was covered with leaves in the summer time, the old, rough Stone said, "Just see how he hides the blue sky from my view!"

And in the winter time when the limbs of the tree were bare, the old, rough Stone said, "Just see how he lets the snow and the cold rain fall right on me!"

One night during a heavy storm the old, rough Stone heard a crash, and in the morning he saw the gnarled tree lying upon the ground. "Now I shall be all by myself again!" he said. Then he counted the rings in the trunk of the gnarled tree until he came to three hundred, which was as far as he could count. "More than three hundred years have passed since that silly little squirrel dropped the nut from which this tree grew!" said the old, rough Stone to himself.

Then men came with axes and cut up the tree and carried all of it away.

When the hot summer days came the sun beat down upon the old, rough Stone and he missed the shade of the gnarled tree. "My! It's hot!" said the old, rough Stone, "I wish the gnarled tree with its pretty rustling leaves were here again to shade me and keep me cool!"

When winter came the old, rough Stone missed the leaves which fell around him and kept him warm.

"Oh dear! How cold it is!" he cried, "I wish the gnarled tree would come back and scatter his leaves about me to protect me from the cold!"

So years and years and years passed, and the great old, rough Stone lay all alone.

"I wish another squirrel would come to eat nuts upon me!" he thought. "Squirrels are such knowing little creatures, I am sure another might drop a nut which would grow into a lovely tree to keep me company."

But, many more years passed, and never again did a tiny squirrel sit upon the old, rough Stone and eat nuts. And never again did another tree grow above the old, rough Stone to keep him company.

"Ah me!" sighed the old, rough Stone, "We never know how well off we are until we lose something we really need!"

SALLY MIGRUNDY

Sally Migrundy lived all alone in a tiny little cottage no larger than a piano box. This was plenty large enough for Sally Migrundy though, for she was a tiny little lady herself. Sally Migrundy's tiny little cottage stood at the edge of a stream, a beautiful crystal clear stream of tinkling water which sang in a continual murmur all day and all night to Sally Migrundy.

The stream tinkled merrily through a great forest which lay for miles and miles, a green mantle over the hills and valleys, and Sally Migrundy's tiny little cottage stood in the exact center of the great whispering forest.

All the wood creatures knew and loved Sally Migrundy and she knew and loved all of the wood creatures.

Each morning she would scatter food upon the surface of the singing stream and the lovely fish, their sides reflecting rainbow colors, would leap from the tinkling waters and splash about to show their pleasure. And she would place food about her little garden for the birds and they in turn repaid her by their wonderful melodies.

Even the mama deer brought their little, wabbly-legged baby deer to introduce to Sally Migrundy; and she rubbed their sleek sides and talked to them so they couldn't but love her.

Now Sally Migrundy had always lived in her tiny cottage on the bank of the tinkling stream which ran through the whispering forest. She had lived there when the largest trees in the forest were tiny little sprouts. She had lived there long before that, and even still longer than that, and that, and that. Ever so much longer!

One day a man who lived on a hill many, many miles away from the whispering forest said to his wife: "Mother, wouldn't you like to know where the water that flows from our spring goes to?" And his wife replied: "It must travel until it reaches the ocean!"

"Yes, I know that, mother" he replied, "but I mean, wouldn't it be interesting to know all of the country through which the water flows?"

So the more they talked of it, the more interested they became until the man finally wrote upon a slip of paper and put the paper into a tiny bottle. Then he put the bottle upon the surface of the spring water and watched it float away.

The little bottle floated along, tumbling over the tiny falls and tinkling ripples and bobbing up and down in the deep, blue, quiet, places until finally it floated to Sally Migrundy's and came to rest in the mass of pretty flowers where Sally Migrundy came each morning to dip her tiny bucket of water.

And so Sally Migrundy found the tiny bottle and took it into her tiny house to read the tiny note she saw inside.

It was such a nice, happy-hearted note Sally Migrundy said: "I will answer it!" So she wrote a happy-hearted note and asked whoever read it to come and visit her. Then she put her note in the tiny bottle and sent it dancing and bobbing down through the whispering forest, riding upon the surface of the singing stream. And Sally Migrundy's note floated along in the bottle until a little boy and a little girl saw it and picked it up.

And when they read Sally Migrundy's happy-hearted note asking them to visit her they started following up the stream until after a long, long time they came to the tiny little cottage.

Sally Migrundy was very much surprised to see the two children, for she had almost forgotten she had written the invitation.

"Howdeedoo!" said Sally Migrundy, "Where in the world did you children come from?"

"We found a note in a bottle and traveled up the stream until we came to your little cottage," they answered.

"But won't your mamas and daddies be worried because you have been away from home so long?" Sally Migrundy asked.

"We are orphans," the children said.

Then Sally Migrundy kissed them and asked them into her tiny cottage.

The door was so small the children had to get down upon their hands and knees to crawl through. But when they got inside they were surprised to find that the rooms were very large. In fact, Sally Migrundy's living room was larger inside than the whole little cottage was on the outside, for, as you have probably guessed, Sally Migrundy's cottage was a magic house.

And in one corner of the living room there was a queer stand with a silver stem sticking up through the center, and the stem curved over and down towards five or six little crystal glasses.

It was a magic soda fountain, as the children soon found out, and they could have all the soda water they wished at any time.

In another room were two little snow white beds. These belonged to them, Sally Migrundy told the children. As you have probably guessed, the magic cottage took care to make everything comfortable for those who came inside.

And when Sally Migrundy had shown the children their pretty bed room she took them to the dining room and there they found a table which had everything nice to eat upon it. And so the children ate and ate and ate, for the magic table knew just what the person wished for who sat at it. So you may be sure there were plenty of cookies and ice cream and candies and golden doughnuts and everything.

So the two little orphan children lived all the time with Sally Migrundy. And each morning when they tumbled, laughing and shouting, out of their little snow white beds, they found underneath a new present. So each morning they had a new toy to play with, for the magic beds knew just what a child would like most each day.

Sally Migrundy was very, very glad the children had come to live with her, so she wrote more notes and sent them down the singing stream, and more and more children came until Sally Migrundy's house was very, very large inside, but still the same tiny little cottage on the outside. The singing and happy laughter of the children echoed through the whispering forest all day, and the ground about the cottage was filled with toys and playthings,—merry-go-rounds, sliding boards, sand piles, hundreds of sand toys, and play houses filled with beautiful dolls and doll furniture.

There was a roller coaster which knew just when to stop and start so that none of the children could ever hurt themselves upon it, and a little play grocery, a little play candy store, and a little play ice cream parlor so that the children could go there at any time and get cookies and candy and ice cream whenever they wished. You may be sure it was a very happy place to live and the children made Sally Migrundy very happy. At first the creatures who lived in the whispering forest were surprised to hear the happy laughter and to see so many children playing about, but they soon grew accustomed to the children and came right up to the grocery and candy store and ice cream parlor to be fed.

Each year Sally Migrundy sends happy-hearted invitations floating down the stream and more orphan children come to live with her. However Sally Migrundy's tiny cottage is just the same tiny cottage on the outside. But when once you crawl through the tiny door, you look upon rows and rows of little rooms, each having one or more little snow white beds in it.

And, while Sally Migrundy remains a tiny little lady only two feet high, she has as much happiness inside as if she were as large as a great big mountain, for as you have probably also guessed, she is a fairy and can have as much room inside for happiness as the little magic cottage could have room inside for all the happy children.

One day the man who lived upon the hill where the spring bubbles up from the ground and makes the beginning of the singing stream said to his wife: "Mother, I will follow the stream and see where it leads to!" So he started down the stream and walked and walked and walked until the stream took him down through the whispering forest clear down to the sea.

Then he turned around and walked back up the stream from the ocean—up through the whispering forest until he came again to his home at the top of the hill.

"I followed the stream down through a great whispering forest, mother," he said, "until I came to the sea. Then I turned around and came back the same way. It was a beautiful trip and when I came to the center of the great whispering forest there was a clearing at the side of the tinkling, singing stream, and the lovely fish leaped from the crystal waters and showed me their wonderful coloring, and the clearing was filled with beautiful flowers and the music of birds. And it was so beautiful I stopped and watched and listened.

"It seemed as if hundreds of children were playing around me, and although I could not hear them yet it seemed to me that I felt they were shouting and laughing at their play!"

"How wonderful it must have been!" said his wife.

"It was indeed very wonderful, mother. And when I returned I again stopped at the same place and sat and listened to the singing of the waters and the birds, and I saw the wild creatures come down into the clearing and act as if they were being fed, and all the time I seemed to feel the laughter and happy shouting of children at play. And a most delightful feeling of contentment and happiness came over me as if I sat within the borders of Fairyland!

"Then as I stooped to drink of the tinkling waters before I started on my way home, I saw, tied to a flower growing in the water, the tiny little bottle with the note inside which I had floated off a long time ago, so I brought it home with me!"

And from his knapsack the man took the tiny bottle and placed it on the table before his wife.

"I wish we knew just who tied the bottle to the flower!" said the wife as she picked the bottle up to look at it. And because the bottle had been used by Sally Migrundy, the two good people suddenly knew all about Sally Migrundy, the magic little cottage, and the happy children who lived there.

Every year the man takes his wife, and together they walk down the tinkling stream until they came to the exact center of the great whispering forest; there they sit for hours at a time, feeling the happiness that overflows from the hearts of Sally Migrundy and the children. And while the good couple have not been able to see the children or Sally Migrundy, or even the tiny magic cottage, they know they are all there, for at times they can hear the laughter and once in a while they feel the touch of a tiny hand. And when they return to their home upon the hill they find they have received enough happiness at the clearing beside the tinkling, singing water to last them for a whole year.

HOW JOHNNY CRICKET SAW SANTA CLAUS

When the first frost came and coated the leaves with its film of sparkles, Mamma Cricket, Papa Cricket, Johnny Cricket and Grandpa Cricket decided it was time they moved into their winter home.

Papa and Mamma and Grandpa Cricket carried all the heavy Cricket furniture, while Johnny Cricket carried the lighter things, such as the family portraits, looking glasses, knives and forks and spoons, and his own little violin.

Aunt Katy Didd wheeled Johnny's little sister Teeny in the Cricket baby buggy and helped Mamma Cricket lay the rugs and wash the stone-work, for you see the Cricket winter home was in the chimney of a big old-fashioned house and the walls were very dusty, and everything was topsy-turvy.

But Mamma Cricket and Aunt Katy Didd soon had everything in tip-top order, and the winter home was just as clean and neat as the summer home out under the rose bush had been.

There the Cricket family lived happily and every thing was just as cozy as any little bug would care to have; on cold nights the people who owned the great big old fashioned house always made a fire in the fireplace, so the walls of the Cricket's winter home were nice and warm, and little Teeny Cricket could play on the floor in her bare feet without fear of catching cold and getting the Cricket croup.

There was one crack in the walls of the Crickets' winter home which opened right into the fireplace, so the light from the fire always lit up the Crickets' living room. Papa Cricket could read the Bugville News while Johnny Cricket fiddled all the latest popular Bug Songs and Mamma Cricket rocked and sang to little Teeny Cricket.

One night, though, the people who owned the great big old fashioned house did not have a fire in the fireplace, and little Teeny Cricket was bundled up in warm covers and rocked to sleep, and all the Cricket family went to bed in the dark.

Johnny Cricket had just dozed into dreamland when he was awakened by something pounding … ever so loudly … and he slipped out of bed and into his two little red topped boots and felt his way to the crack in the living room wall.

Johnny heard loud voices and merry peals of laughter, so he crawled through the crack and looked out into the fireplace.

There in front of the fireplace he saw four pink feet and two laughing faces way above, while just a couple of Cricket-hops from Johnny's nose was a great big man. Johnny could not see what the man was pounding, but he made an awful loud noise.

Finally the pounding ceased and the man leaned over and kissed the owners of the pink feet. Then there were a few more squeals of laughter, and the four pink feet pitter-patted across the floor and Johnny could see the owners hop into a snow-white bed.

Then Johnny saw the man walk to the lamp and turn the light down low, and leave the great big room.

Johnny Cricket jumped out of the crack into the fireplace and ran out into the great big room so that he might see what the man had pounded. The light from the lamp was too dim for him to make out the objects hanging from the mantel above the fireplace. All he could see were four long black things, so Johnny Cricket climbed up the bricks at the side of the fireplace until he came to the mantel shelf, then he ran along the shelf and looked over. The black things were stockings.

Johnny began to wish that he had stopped to put on his stockings, for he was in his bare feet. He had removed his little red topped boots when he decided to climb up the side of the fireplace and now his feet were cold.

So Johnny started to climb over the mantel shelf and down the side of the fireplace when there came a puff of wind down the chimney which made the stockings swing away out into the room, and snowflakes fluttered clear across the room.

There was a tiny tinkle from a bell and, just as Johnny hopped behind the clock, he saw a boot stick out of the fireplace.

Then Johnny Cricket's little bug heart went pitty-pat, and sounded as if it would run a race with the ticking of the clock.

From his hiding place, Johnny Cricket heard one or two chuckles, and something rattle. Johnny crept along the edge of the clock and holding the two feelers over his back looked from his hiding place....

At first all he could see were two hands filling the stockings with rattly things, but when the hands went down below the mantel for more rattly things, Johnny Cricket saw a big round smiling face all fringed with snow-white whiskers.

Johnny drew back into the shadow of the clock, and stayed there until the rattling had ceased and all had grown quiet, then he slipped from behind the clock and climbed down the side of the fireplace as fast as he could. Johnny Cricket was too cold to stop and put on his little red boots, but scrambled through the crack in the fireplace and hopped into bed. In the morning Mamma Cricket had a hard time getting Johnny Cricket out of bed. He yawned and stretched, put on one stocking, rubbed his eyes, yawned, put on another stocking and yawned again. Johnny was still very sleepy and could hardly keep his eyes open as he reached for his little red-toppedboots.

Johnny's toe struck something hard, he yawned, rubbed his eyes and looked into the boot. Yes, there was something in Johnny Cricket's boot! He picked up the other boot; it, too, had something in it!

It was candy! With a loud cry for such a little Cricket, Johnny rushed to the kitchen and showed Mamma, then he told her of his adventure of the night before.

Mamma Cricket called Papa and they both had a laugh when Johnny told how startled he had been at the old man with the white whiskers who filled the stockings in front of the fireplace. "Why, Johnny!" said Mamma and Papa Cricket. "Don't you know? That was Santa Claus. We have watched him every Christmas in the last four years fill the stockings, and he saw your little red topped boots and filled them with candy, too. If you will crawl through the crack into the fireplace you will see the children of the people who own this big house playing with all the presents that Santa Claus left them!"

And, sure enough, it was so!

THE TWIN SISTERS

Everybody in the little village called them the twin houses because they were built exactly alike. But the two little cottages looked different even if they were built alike, for one was covered with climbing vines and beautiful scarlet roses while the other had no vines or flowers about it at all.

Everybody called the two cottages the twin houses for another reason: the owners were twins. One of the twins was Matilda and the other Katrinka and they were as much alike on the outside as their two cottages were alike; but as their two cottages differed, so did the two twins differ.

Matilda could not be told from Katrinka should you just see them walking down the street, but the minute either of them spoke you would know which was Matilda and which was Katrinka. Matilda, who lived in the bare cottage, was sour and disagreeable, while Katrinka was happy and cheery.

So the people in the little village called Matilda "Matilda Grouch" and they called Katrinka "Katrinka Sunshine". All the children of the little village loved Katrinka, for she always had a cooky or a dainty in her apron pocket to give them, or she would pat them on their curly heads and smile cheerily at them through her glasses. And all the children avoided Matilda, for, sometimes mistaking her for Katrinka and running close to greet her, they would have their noses tweeked for their trouble.

Matilda's life was lonely and cold; no one went to see her. She was always unhappy.

Katrinka's house always echoed with the laughter of children; everyone went to see her. She was always joyful and cheery.

One night while Matilda sat at her dark window looking across at Katrinka's house, she saw a crowd of people tip-toeing up to the stoop with baskets under their arms and flowers in their hands and when all had crowded upon the porch they stamped their feet and made a great noise.

Matilda was very angry, but Katrinka ran laughing to the door and greeted all with her kindliest smile. It was a surprise party for Katrinka, for it was her birthday.

Matilda watched the party from her dark window and the longer she watched, the more angry she grew, for the longer the party lasted, the louder grew the happy laughter.

Finally when all the guests had gone, Matilda saw Katrinka gather up half of the presents and put them in a basket.

Then Katrinka stole softly up to Matilda's stoop and stamped her feet. Matilda sat scowling by the dark window a long time before she finally went to the door, for she was very peevish.

"This is a fine time to come stamping upon a person's stoop!" she scolded, as Katrinka walked into the living room.

"Oh, sister," Katrinka cried, as she tried to kiss Matilda. "This is our birthday and I have brought you half of the presents which were given me! See?" and she piled the presents high upon the table.

"I do not wish them!" said Matilda, frowning at her sister. But Katrinka could see that Matilda *did* wish them.

"The presents were not for me, Katrinka!" she said.

"Oh yes they are!" Katrinka replied. "They were given to me and I give them to you! I have saved one half for myself! But you should have been to the party!" said Katrinka, "We had such a happy time!"

"I do not enjoy being with people!" Matilda scolded, "I wish to be left to myself!"

"Yes, but Matilda," her sister said, "you do not know the happiness in being kind and friendly to others!"

"Pooh!" sniffed Matilda.

"I just wish you could take my place and know the happiness that is in my heart tonight," Katrinka smiled.

"I just wish you could take my place and know the unhappiness that is in my heart tonight!" said Matilda, "You would see that a lot of children screeching about the house with all their presents could not bring me happiness!"

Katrinka thought a moment, "I have it, Matilda! We will change places! You must live in my house and pretend that you are me, and I will live in your house and pretend that I am you! And you must smile and be friendly just as I would do."

After a great deal of coaxing, Matilda finally agreed that she would change places with Katrinka and try to smile when anyone came to see her.

"But only for three days!" she said.

So Matilda went over to Katrinka's cottage and went to bed and Katrinka stayed in Matilda's cottage, but she did not go to bed.

Instead she went all over the house and tidied everything up and placed pretty white curtains at the windows. In the morning neighbors came to Katrinka's house, and Matilda, taking Katrinka's place met them with a smile, and soon in spite of herself she was laughing and enjoying herself.

And when they left, Matilda felt that she enjoyed having them there.

But what was the callers' surprise when they passed Matilda's cottage to see someone planting flowers around the stoop. They stopped in wonderment and, as Katrinka looked up at them with a cheery "Good Morning!" and a happy smile they could scarce believe their eyes and ears, for they thought it was Matilda.

And these callers told other neighbors and they called at Katrinka's house and visited with Matilda and Matilda was so pleased she laughed as cheerily as Katrinka could laugh. And as the neighbors left they saw Katrinka in Matilda's front yard planting flowers and stopped in open mouthed wonder to gaze at her, for *they* thought she was Matilda.

And when Katrinka smiled at them and said her cheery "Good morning" *they* could scarcely believe their eyes and ears.

The neighbors all put their heads together, and that evening they filled their baskets with goodies and presents and, with large bouquets of flowers, they tiptoed up to Matilda's front stoop and stamped their feet.

Now Katrinka had called Matilda over to her own house to see the changes she had made and Matilda was beginning to see what she had missed all along. And as they were talking, there came a noise at the front stoop.

"Shall I go to the door, Matilda?" asked Katrinka.

"No, I will go, Katrinka!" Matilda replied, her face alight with happiness. So Matilda welcomed her guests as cheerily as Katrinka had done the evening before and the laughter lasted until 'way in the night.

And when the last guest had left, Matilda took Katrinka in her arms and said, "I will not need to change places with you again, Katrinka, for I have found that there is far more pleasure in being happy than in being unhappy!" "Of course there is, Matilda!" Katrinka replied. "You see, in order to be happy ourselves we must reflect happiness to others, and the more cheer we give to others the more joy we receive ourselves, so we must continue to change from one house to another every other day so that no one will know which of us is Matilda and which is Katrinka and we will share our happiness with each other."

So Matilda's house was soon surrounded with beautiful flowers and her house echoed with the fun and laughter of happy children.

And the two sisters who looked alike now acted alike and could not be told apart, and they changed about so often people never knew whether they were visiting Katrinka or whether they were visiting Matilda, for one was as cheery as the other and was as happy in the love of all the people in the little village.

And, as they could not be told apart, everyone called Matilda or Katrinka the Cheery Twins whenever they spoke of either.

LITTLE THUMBKIN'S GOOD DEED

Thumbkins lived in a tiny, cozy little house right down beneath a mushroom. The tiny, little house was made of cobwebs which Thumbkins had gathered from the bushes and weeds. These he had woven together with thistle-down, making the nicest little nest imaginable.

One day Thumbkins was passing through the meadow and it began to rain. "Dear me! I shall get soaking wet!" Thumbkins cried as he hurried along.

A mamma meadow-lark, sitting upon her nest, saw Thumbkins running and called to him: "Come here, little man, and get beneath my wing and I will keep you warm and dry!"

So Thumbkins crawled beneath Mamma Meadow-Lark's wings and, snuggling down close to the bottom of the meadow-lark's nest, he found three tiny little baby meadow-larks. It was too dark for Thumbkins to see them, but he felt that the baby Meadow-Larks were as warm as toast.

Thumbkins kept very quiet, for the baby meadow-larks were sleepy little fellows, and before he knew it Thumbkins was sound asleep himself, with an arm around one of the baby birds.

Thumbkins did not know how long he had been asleep, but when he awakened the rain had ceased. Thumbkins knew it had stopped raining for he could no longer hear the rain drops pattering upon Mamma Meadow-Lark's back. So now he climbed out of the nest and looked about.

The ground about the Meadow-Lark's nest was covered with tiny puddles, and Mamma Meadow-Lark was soaking wet. She looked very uncomfortable. Her feathers stuck out in all directions and a drop of water fell from her head and rolled down her beak.

Thumbkins thought at first Mamma Meadow-Lark was crying, and he said: "Are you cold, Mamma Meadow-Lark?"

"Yes, indeed!" Mamma Meadow-Lark replied as she shook her ruffled feathers, sending the water flying in all directions.

"But, you see," she continued, "if I did not cover my baby Meadow-Lark chicks they would get very, very cold, for they have little bald heads with not a single feather upon them to protect them! So, while I get wet, it does not matter so much, for I know I have kept my little Meadow-Lark chicks dry and warm and cozy and that, of course, makes me very happy! And I had the pleasure of keeping you warm and dry, too!" Mamma Meadow-Lark added.

"Perhaps Mamma Meadow-Lark is very happy inside!" Thumbkins thought to himself as he stood and looked at her. "But she does not look very happy with such wet feathers."

"I thank you ever and ever so much, Mamma Meadow-Lark!" Thumbkins said.

"You are indeed very welcome," Mamma Meadow-Lark replied, "and any time it rains you can come back to my nest and crawl beneath my wing and keep warm and dry. For you are tiny and do not take up much room!"

Thumbkins thanked Mamma Meadow-Lark again, and told her of his nice warm cozy little nest beneath the mushroom. "It is always nice and dry there," he said, "for the rain runs right off the mushroom and does not touch my little cobweb home!"

That night as he lay in his little thistle-down bed, Thumbkins heard it thundering. "I'm very glad that I haven't a home built right out upon the bare ground like the meadow-larks!" he said. And as the thunder grew louder, Thumbkins turned over and tried to go to sleep.

Presently the raindrops began to patter on the round top of the mushroom and "drip-dropped" to the ground without getting Thumbkins' little house the least bit wet. Usually when it rained, the patter of the raindrops upon his mushroom roof lulled Thumbkins right to sleep, but tonight Thumbkins lay wide awake and thought and thought.

"I can't go to sleep!" Thumbkins said, so he hopped out of his warm little bed and lit his tiny lantern. Then, though it was raining ever so hard, he pulled his little hat well down on his head and ran out into the storm.

Yes! There was Mamma Meadow-Lark sitting upon her nest with her head tucked under her wing, sound asleep. But when he held his tiny lantern close, Thumbkins could see that she shivered as the cold raindrops splashed upon her back.

So Thumbkins ran to the woods where he knew the mushrooms grew, and breaking off the largest one he could find he carried it to where Mamma Meadow-Lark sat sleeping upon her nest, and planted it so the raindrops rolled off the round roof and did not touch her at all.

Then, shivering himself, for he was soaking wet, he ran home as fast as he could, took off his dripping clothes, put on his little pajamas, and climbed into his warm little cozy cobweb bed.

Now of course Thumbkins was happy because he had helped another, and when a person is happy there is nothing to worry about, and when there is nothing to worry about, of course there is nothing to keep one awake.

So Thumbkins fell fast asleep and dreamed the most pleasant dreams.

And they were such happy dreams Thumbkins slept until almost half-past eight the next morning.

THE WISHBONE

The stove lifter lay upon his iron side and looked across the top of the shelf which stood above the stove. "Who is he?" he asked of the box of matches lying near him.

The box of matches looked at the strange new object standing upon two thin white legs and leaning against the wall near the coffee pot.

"I do not know!" the match box answered.

Then they asked a number of other objects lying about if they knew who the newcomer was, but none of them had ever seen anything like him before.

When the new two-legged object with the bald head heard everyone whispering he felt they were talking about him, and he stepped out where all might see him, and walked up and down the shelf at the back of the stove.

The stove lifter, the match box and all the other objects watched him with interest as he strutted back and forth.

At last the new object stood still and with his head thrown back he said: "I am a wish-bone, but as none of you know what a wishbone is, I shall tell you! A wishbone is an object of great importance in this world. Some of us come from the breasts of chickens and some from the breasts of turkeys. When we are placed above a doorsill in a house, we bring good luck!"

"Don't the people in the house here wish good luck?" asked the match box.

"What a silly question!" replied the wishbone, "Anyone could easily see you do not know much!"

"Then why didn't they place you above the door?" asked the stove lifter.

"Because I have greater qualities than bringing good luck!" the wishbone answered. "The children placed me here to dry, for they have heard that I make wishes come true! And if you keep your eyes and ears open you will see just what a great object a wishbone really is!"

All the other objects upon the shelf on the back of the stove held their breaths to think such an important object deigned to talk to them.

Then the children came romping into the kitchen. "Here they come!" cried the wishbone. "Now watch me make their wishes come true!"

And all the other objects scarcely breathed while they watched the children as they took the wishbone from the shelf. They could see how proud he looked as the children each took one of the wishbone's legs between their fingers.

"I wish that this kitchen were just filled with candy and cake, then we could eat all we wish to!" one of the children said. "And I wish for a million golden pennies piled high upon the kitchen table!" the other child cried.

"Now watch!" the wishbone winked to the objects upon the shelf behind the stove.

The two children pulled upon the wishbone's legs. "Ouch!" he cried. There was a loud snap, and the wishbone broke in two.

"I get my Wish!" cried the child with the longest part of the broken wishbone, "The room will be filled with candy!"

"Watch the room fill with candy!" cried all the objects upon the shelf. "How wonderful it must be to be a wishbone!"

But the room did not fill with candy.

"That's another time the wish did not come true!" cried one child.

"They never come true!" cried the other child as the broken wishbone was tossed in the coal scuttle. "Wishbones are just ordinary bones and do not make wishes come true!" And the children ran outside to romp and play.

"How much better it is to be a useful object!" said the stove lifter.

"Yes indeed!" replied the match box. "And the more useful one is, usually, the less he brags about himself!"

TIM TIM TAMYTAM

"This looks like an excellent place, Tim Tim!" Mrs. Tamytam said, as she threw her little poke bonnet back from her head. "An excellent place!" Tim Tim Tamytam scrambled up the root of the tree and peered into the dark hole in the tree trunk. "HMMM!" he said by way of reply, "Did you bring the candle with you, Tum Tum?"

"Oh, I forgot it, Tim Tim!" his little wife replied, "I will run right back and get it!"

"No, Tum Tum! I will run home and get it! You sit down upon this soft little toad-stool and wait until I return. It will take me but a moment!"

So Mrs. Tamytam sat down to wait upon the little soft toad-stool, with her bonnet hanging over her shoulders, and she sang and knitted.

Now, Mrs. Tamytam was a delightful little elfish lady, and she and Tim Tim were very, very happy together, even though they were only six inches tall.

So, while she sang and knitted, Tim Tim ran down the tiny path made by the woodfolk, past the bubbling spring and around the bend in the bank of the tumbling brooklet until he came to his home, which was another hole in the trunk of an old tree.

As Tim Tim climbed into his doorway, he stood and looked with dismay at what had been his cozy living room, for now it was filled with sawdust and small pieces of sticks and twigs, for the whole top of the old tree had broken off and now the rain would splash right down on everything the first time there was a shower.

Tim Tim Tamytam searched about in the sawdust and twigs until he found a tiny bit of bayberry candle, and, putting this in his pocket, he turned to go out of the hole. But just then Tom Tom Teenyweeny walked in the door.

"Hello, Tom Tom Teenyweeny!" Tim Tim cried cheerily.

"Hello, Tim Tim Tamytam!" Tom Tom cried at the same time, "What ever has happened to your lovely home, Tim Tim?"

"Well, I will tell you, Tom Tom," Tim Tim answered, "You know Mrs. Fuzzytail lived with her grandchildren squirrels up in the top of the tree, and they had a very cozy den up there, too, but Mrs. Fuzzytail wished to make some small improvements, such as a new peep-hole window and a little cupboard for Chinkapins and hickory nuts. So last summer she sent for the carpenter ants and arranged with them to do the carpenter work. And do you know, Tom Tom," and here Tim Tim Tamytam put his hand upon Tom Tom's shoulder and got very confidential, "those mischievous carpenter ants, when they once got started, they sawed and chipped, until they had cut almost all of the shell of the tree away, and when it blew so very hard last night the top of the tree broke right in two, where the ants had made their tunnels, and down it fell with a great crash and made this great pile of sawdust and sticks!" "Dear me!" said Tom Tom. "Was anyone hurt when the top of the tree fell?"

"Fortunately no one was injured!" Tim Tim replied, "But our home was ruined and so was Mrs. Fuzzytail's and Wally Woodpecker's, the bachelor and we have been out looking for another home. If you will come with me, Tom Tom, I will show it to you, for now I have a candle and can look about inside!"

So Tim Tim and Tom Tom ran back along the tiny wood-folk path until they came to the place where Tim Tim had left Mrs. Tamytam.

There hung her knitting bag upon the stem of a flower, but Tum Tum Tamytam was no where about.

"OOOHooooo!" Tim Tim called, putting his hands to his mouth and forming a sort of horn. Charley Chipmunk stopped whittling upon a hickory nut and peeped over the limb to see who called.

Mrs. Tamytam did not answer, so Tom Tom took a leaf and rolled it into a horn. Across the small end he strung a fibre from a piece of moss and with this elfin horn he blew the Tim Tim Tamytam wood-call: "Tahoo Tahoo Tahoo-hoo-hoo!"

"That's the Tim Tim Tamytam call!" all the wood creatures, said, as they listened.

"Tahoo Tahoo Tahoo-hoo-hoo!"

And as Tim Tim and Tom Tom listened, they heard away off the answering Tamytam wood-call: "Toowoo-toowoo-tooawoooooo!" sounding like the plaintive notes of the turtle dove but was easily distinguished by any of the woodfolk.

Tim Tim and Tom Tom followed the sound of the answering call until they came to a beautiful woodland glade. There, where the sweet ferns and fragrant flowers grew in profusion and a carpet of velvety moss spread upon the ground, they saw Mrs. Tom Tom Teenyweeny and Mrs. Tim Tim Tamytam with tiny brooms sweeping out a little hole in a great blue-gray beech tree.

"I came upon Mrs. Tamytam sitting upon the toad stool," said Mrs. Teenyweeny, "and as I had just heard of this lovely home for rent, she came with me to see it and we decided to take it!"

"And will Tom Tom and Mrs. Teenyweeny live with us, Tum Tum?" Tim Tim asked.

"They have the little nook right across the hall!" Mrs. Tamytam replied. Upon hearing this Tom Tom and Tim Tim caught hold of hands and danced about, kicking up their heels with pleasure.

"Just wait until you see inside, Tom Tom and Tim Tim!" Mrs. Teenyweeny and Mrs. Tamytam cried, and then they led the way inside the trunk of the great blue-gray beech tree.

And after they had inspected Mrs. Tamytam's home, Mrs. Teenyweeny's Tom Tom and Tim Tim were as delighted with the new homes as their tiny wives had been, so Tim Tim and Tom Tom ran to their old homes and brought all their furniture and placed it about the large living rooms.

When all was finished and the tiny rugs had been placed just right, they heard a stamping of tiny feet in the hallway.

And as they ran to the door a merry, laughing crowd of tiny creatures like themselves, each carrying an acorn basket, trooped into the living room.

"It's a surprise party!" they all shouted and then one, Tee Tee Tubbytee, a great speaker, said: "We watched you moving in, and decided to have a nice, fine, lovely party for you, so I called all the neighbors together and here we are!"

Some of the tiny creatures had brought their tiny violins and some their elfin flutes, and as all were in a merry mood they played rollicking airs such as "The Wind Tinkles the Fairy Bells" and "Mother Hulda Picks Her Geese."

Tim Tim and Tom Tom danced and sang elfin songs. And then the merry tiny creatures ate the goodies brought in the acorn baskets.

After the dinner all the tiny creatures went outside, and upon the soft, mossy carpet they held a wood-folk dance while the silvery moon peeped down through the leaves of the woodland glade and bathed the scene in fairy light.

When the first rooster crowed, far away in a distant farm yard chicken coop, the tiny creatures, after planning another surprise party the next moonlit night, bade each other good night and went to their tree trunk homes.

So upon soft summer evenings, should you pass near the woodland glade, you may hear the "Tahoo Tahoo Tahoo-hoo-hoo!" and the answering notes of plaintive melody, "Toowoo-toowoo Tooawoooooo!" For the tiny creatures have adopted the Tamytam call as the call to the evening parties. And you must step quietly and approach softly so as not to disturb the tiny creatures, when you wish to see one of their moonlight surprise parties.

A CHANGE OF COATS

Two mischievous little gnomes were walking along the beach one day and as they came to a pile of rocks they heard voices. One of the little gnomes put his finger to his lips for silence and peeped cautiously around the largest stone. There he saw a crab and a lobster sitting upon a bunch of sea-weed in the sunshine.

The other little gnome tip-toed up and joined his brother and when they had listened a while they winked at each other and quietly walked back to the beach. After whispering together a moment one of the little gnomes ran up the beach and over a sand dune.

The other gnome again crept up behind the large stone and listened to the lobster and the crab.

"Yes," said the crab, "I agree with you, Mr. Lobster! While our coats are just a plain green they are still quite beautiful!"

"Ah! You speak the truth, Friend Crab," the lobster replied, "Green is a lovely color and I am very glad that we are not purple!"

"I am very glad that we are green, too." the crab said, "Just suppose we were colored blue! I know I should not be able to stand it! Would you, Friend Lobster?'

"No indeed!" the lobster cried, "Nor would I care to change to any other color, would you, Friend Crab!" "It is nice to be satisfied! Isn't it, Friend Lobster?"

"Yes! Especially when we are as satisfied as we are!" The lobster answered.

The little gnome listening behind the large stone winked at himself and smiled. He knew the lobster and the crab would give anything if they were of a different color, for he could tell by their conversation they were dissatisfied with their green coats.

Soon the other little gnome appeared over the sand dunes carrying a large kettle, and when he got to a spot on the beach where the crab and the lobster could see and hear him he began shouting in a sing-song manner: "Old clothes changed to new! Old clothes changed to new! Old clothes changed to new!"

"Pooh!" said the lobster. "Who is foolish enough to wish to change their natural coats?"

"Hmm!" said the crab as he sidled towards the beach. "Let's go over and talk with him, anyway, and ask him if anyone ever changes the color of their clothes. Not that I wish to change my lovely green coat, you understand, but —"

"It would be interesting to hear about it, anyway!" the lobster replied, as he crawled after the crab.

The little gnome with the large kettle sat upon the beach and pretended he did not see the crab and lobster, but continued crying: "Old coats changed to new! Green ones changed to red! Old coat changed to new! Old coats changed to new!"

When the crab and the lobster came up quite near the little gnome pulled a number of pieces of colored cloth from his pocket and placed them upon the sand.

"How pretty!" said the crab.

"Very lovely!" said the lobster.

"Do you wish your coats changed in color?" asked the little gnome.

"Ah, no, thank you!" the two hypocrites said. "We were just looking around a bit!"

"Well, I am glad to have your company," said the little gnome as he took a piece of scarlet cloth and laid it over the lobster's back.

"How do you like that?" he asked of the crab.

"It looks fine!" said the crab. "Try it on me!"

The little gnome placed the scarlet piece of cloth over the crab's back.

"How do you like it?" he asked the lobster.

"Did I look that well in that color?" asked the lobster by way of reply.

"I think both of you will look far better if you let me change you to scarlet. It's in far better taste, too!" the little gnome added, pinching himself to keep from laughing.

"Shall we change?" the crab asked the lobster and the lobster asked the crab.

"You will find the color a great deal warmer," said the little gnome. "Green is decidedly cold, you know!"

So the little gnome gathered an armful of drift-wood and built a fire. Then he dipped the kettle into the sea and placed the crab and the lobster in the kettle of water and put the lid on.

"Be sure and make us a brilliant scarlet!" cried the lobster and the crab, as the little gnome placed the kettle over the fire. An hour later the two little gnomes lay upon their backs upon the sand and yawned contentedly, their little round stomachs almost bursting their belts. Near them was the upturned kettle, and scattered all about them on the sand were lovely pieces of scarlet lobster and crab shells.

"It's funny," one little gnome said drowsily, "how one sometimes will become dissatisfied with the way he was made by Mother Nature and try to improve upon her work! It usually leads to misfortune."

"Yes, that is true," the other little gnome replied, "We should be satisfied and contented just as we are!"

"Well, I for one am satisfied!" the little gnome said, stroking his fat stomach.

"So am I!" his brother laughed.

[Click on the End-Papers to enlarge to full size.]

Lightning Source UK Ltd.
Milton Keynes UK
UKHW010050011022
409740UK00002B/52